The Heroes of
Castle Lovat

Elkie Kammer

Printed by
For The Right Reasons
38-40 Grant Street, Inverness, IV3 8BN
Email: fortherightreasons@rocketmail.com
Tel:01463 237969 or 07717457247

The Heroes of Castle Lovat

Content

1) Too Much Noise

Danny's head began to spin. He was trying hard to listen to the teacher, but there were so many other voices around him, making it hard to concentrate. Chairs scraping on the floor, people whispering to each other, someone sharpening a pencil and someone sniffling with a cold. On top of all these noises came the screaming of words and pictures from the walls. Adjectives, 3D shapes, class rules, world religions, star writers, times tables, children's portraits, a list of common words and to top it all, models of the planets dangling from a washing line across the room.

Danny tried hard to block it all out and focus his attention on what the teacher was saying. He got the first instruction and the second, but after that his head seemed fit to burst. When Kyle nudged him and asked to borrow his rubber, Danny exploded.

"Get your own rubber!" he shouted, pushing Kyle away. It might have ended there, had the classroom assistant not stepped in at that moment.

"Danny, that's your first warning. You know hitting is not allowed in here", she said in a calm voice, but to Danny it sounded like the roar of a tiger. It was the last drop to tip him over the edge.

"Shut up! I'm trying to concentrate!" he yelled at the woman, banging his fist on the table.

Danny!" came the shout of the teacher in the suddenly quiet classroom. "How dare you speak to Miss Cotswold like that!"

He didn't hear what else she was saying, as her words suddenly became a stream of unintelligible sounds, hurting his ears and his head and his whole being. He jumped up, kicking his chair over and made for the door to get out. If only Sarah's gym bag hadn't tripped him up! That was the end. Danny just lost it. He hurled the gym bag right across the room with the most bloodcurdling scream, before grabbing her chair and tipping her onto the floor. Hassid, who sat next to Sarah, jumped up in fear and was rewarded with a blow from Danny's fist. He no longer knew what he was doing. He was like a wild animal in panic mode, fighting for its life. His arms swept over the tabletops, sending jotters, books and pencils in all directions. Chairs were kicked and children punched and the planets came off their line, crashing through space and bouncing off the walls.

By the time Miss Cotswold and the teacher were upon him, Danny's energy was spent. He lay in a heap on the floor with his hands over his ears, rocking and moaning softly. Fortunately, they didn't make it worse by shouting at him or touching him. Instead, the teacher opened the classroom door and made sure his path was unobstructed. Her gesture was clear. He was free to escape. With the last of his strength Danny got to his feet and walked out. As if by themselves, his legs took him to his hiding place in the cloakroom, where he squeezed in the corner under the bench.

It was Katie, who found him there later. Danny had calmed down by then, but he felt too embarrassed to go back to class.

"It's nearly break time", Katie said, looking out of the window. "You'd better come out before it gets busy in here." With that she left him to make his own decision.

Danny waited until her footsteps disappeared in the corridor. Then he crawled out of his hiding place, took his jacket off the hook and his snack out of his bag and made for the playground before the noise of the bell could hurt his ears.

2) Misunderstandings

Katie had always understood him best and Danny was glad to have her in his class. She didn't have an easy time either and got into trouble at least as much as he did.

After break, the teacher called Danny aside and made him apologise to Miss Cotswold and to Hassid and Sarah. She also explained that he was on 30 minutes detention during lunch hour in order to catch up with the work he had missed.

Danny couldn't stop worrying about it. He didn't think he was able to remember what the teacher had explained before he had *lost it*. And what about needing to de-stress? It was part of his routine to run along the playground fence after he had eaten his lunch, letting his hands flap and his voice express whatever sounds were bubbling out of him. Danny knew that he needed that time if he was to last for the rest of the school day.

The worries were nagging away at him, leaving no room for whatever it was they were meant to find out in their books. He had almost made up his mind to simply run away, when the class suddenly fell silent. Everybody's eyes were directed at Katie. She was standing in the library corner with an open book in one hand and a ripped out page in the other. On the windowsill behind her were more loose pages.

"What on earth has come into you, Katie!" the teacher's voice broke the silence. She was as stunned as everyone else in the room.

Katie looked confused. "You told us to extract information and extract means to take out", she said as if explaining the obvious. "I extracted five or six pages of useful information for my project." She turned to the windowsill and picked up the other sheets.

"Are you trying to make fun of me?" the teacher asked angrily.
"No, why?" Katie replied, genuinely puzzled.
"For goodness sake, do you really think I would ask you to wreck our library books for your project?" The teacher went on.

Katie considered this for a moment, before she said: "Well, I thought it was crazy of you, but you did say *extract* and it means *to take out.*" While Katie remained as calm as a cucumber, the teacher was fuming.
"How dare you speak to me like that!" she shouted. "You are old enough to know that extracting information does not mean ripping brand new books apart!"

Katie studied the cover of the book she was holding. "This isn't brand new", she said matter-of-fact. She opened the cover. "It says here it was published in 2005."

A few children began to giggle and to roll their eyes, whispering to each other, which made the teacher's temper even worse.
"Stop acting so smart!" she bellowed at Katie. "If you cannot show respect for this school and its property, you might as well leave and seek your education elsewhere!" With that, she turned round and walked back to the white-board.

"Leave?" Katie asked incredulously.
"Yes, *leave* as in *get out*", the boy closest to her said earnestly. So Katie put the

book down and walked to the door. The other children started shuffling and their voices rose. The teacher still had her back to them and seemed unsure how to face the class again. She finally looked at the clock and took a deep breath.

"Right, children", she said at last, turning slowly towards them. "It's almost lunch time. Stop what you're doing and tidy up."

Danny stared at the empty page in his jotter. He hadn't been able to extract any information for his project and the prospect of lunchtime detention nearly choked him. Then he thought of Katie, who had been thrown out of class and perhaps even out of school. Suddenly he had an idea. In the hustle and bustle of tidying up he quietly slipped out into the corridor and hurried to the cloakroom.

Katie was still there, dressed in her coat and outdoor shoes and zipping up her bag.

"Where are you going?" Danny asked her. "Home, I think", she answered. "Only my mum won't be there yet and I don't have a key." She looked rather unsure.
"We could just go to the woods by the Community Centre", Danny suggested.
"You and me?" Katie asked.
"Yes", Danny answered. "I don't want to go to lunchtime detention." He took his jacket off the hook and quickly changed his shoes. Then the two of them followed the corridor to the school entrance, where they sneaked past the secretary's office and out into the street.

3) Playing truant

First they were excited to be out of school in the middle of the day. Danny's hands wouldn't stop flapping and he talked non-stop about all kinds of random things. Katie just giggled, saying over and over again "She told me to leave."

In the woods they were sheltered from the cold wind and felt save from prying eyes, but soon they realised that they missed their lunch.

"I'm hungry", Katie announced when they came to a clearing with moss covered tree trunks.

"So am I", Danny agreed. "We should've stayed until after we'd eaten." He sat down on one of the tree trunks and started plucking at the grass by his feet.

"Maybe we find some berries", Katie suggested, looking around for something edible.

"Not at this time of year", Danny put in. "Berries only grow in summer and autumn."

"Then maybe mushrooms", Katie said hopefully.

"We can't cook them", Danny replied. "And we can't eat them raw."

Katie sighed. She kicked at a rotten branch that had come off a tree. "What about your house?"

Danny shook his head. "My dad would take us straight back to school."

"But I was told to leave!" Katie shouted. "They wouldn't let me back in!"

Danny jumped up. "I'm getting cold sitting here." He rubbed his hands together and stamped his feet. "Let's move on. Perhaps we come up with an idea."

For the next hour or so they kept walking around in the woods. It was a peaceful place and they both began to relax. They even glimpsed a roe deer that was crossing their path.

"I wish I was a deer", Katie said. "Then I could live in the woods and eat grass and berries with nobody shouting at me."

"But you might get shot", Danny warned her. "Or you're eaten by a fox."

"And I wouldn't be able to read books", Katie said sadly. She loved reading and she loved maths even more. Unlike Danny, she actually loved school, if only the teachers wouldn't talk in riddles half of the time. The other day she had been told off for sitting on the teacher's padded swivel chair, although they had been told to "sit wherever you like". And then there was the row she had got for kicking a rubber under the bookshelf. "You said to put it back where I found it", Katie had answered in defence, "and I found it under there."

"Don't be cheeky!" the teacher had hissed at her like a poisonous snake.

Once Katie couldn't resist telling her what she sounded like, causing the teacher to fly into a rage. Katie had to put her hands over her ears to cope with the noise she made. As usual, she didn't understand what she had done to make the teacher so angry. What could be wrong with telling the truth?

Danny stopped in his tracks. Katie nearly bumped into him. "What's wrong?" she asked.

"Shsh!" Danny whispered. "Someone's coming." He beckoned Katie to follow him into a thicket.

"Why do we have to hide?" she wanted to know.

"Because it could be a junky or a child molester", Danny explained. They waited silently for the footsteps to come closer. Through the twigs and pine needles they spotted an old man with a small dog by his side. He would probably have walked right past them, if the dog hadn't caught their scent. It pricked up its ears and stopped. Then it barked at the thicket they were hiding in.

"No chasing squirrels!" the old man said sternly, but the dog stood its ground, growling and barking. Suddenly it rushed forward and Katie jumped in fright. The man saw her and called his dog to heel.

"What are you doing out here, young lady?" he asked, fastening the lead on the dog's collar. That's when Danny decided to stand up. He didn't trust Katie to come up with a good enough excuse.

"We're collecting leaves and cones for a school project," he answered quickly. "We even found an empty bird's nest, but we left it in case the birds come back." Danny was good at making up stories, so good that he often believed what he was telling.

"Ah, a school project!" The old man nodded. "I remember pressing colourful leaves as a boy, but at this time of year everything is brown and rotten." The dog strained at the lead, whining and wagging its tail.

"Yes, that makes them more interesting", Danny explained, picking up a mushy leaf. "You can see the vanes inside and how they crumble and turn into earth." He rubbed the leaf between his fingers and let the bits sail to the ground.

"Alright", the old man chuckled. "You get on with your project then and make sure to get back to school before the bell rings!" He turned and pulled the dog after him, leaving Katie and Danny to ponder their encounter.

"I would have liked to stroke the dog", Katie said, while she was climbing out of the thicket. "It looked really cute."
Danny wasn't sure it would have been a good idea. "It could have bitten you", he put in, "and anyway, the man could've been a baddy, trying to kidnap you. Remember: Never trust a stranger."

They walked on for a while, but soon got bored. As peaceful as the woods were, they didn't provide much of interest at this time of year.

"Maybe it's time to go home now", Katie suggested.

"I don't think so", Danny replied. "We haven't been here for that long."

"I'm still hungry", Katie announced.

"Yea, we should've had school dinner before we left", Danny agreed. For a while they talked about their favourite food, which for Danny consisted of macaroni cheese and plain custard and for Katie of vegetable soup. Once they had exhausted this topic, they fell silent, walking on, each in their own thoughts.

4) Caught

The old man must have given them away, or perhaps the police would have found them anyway. When Katie and Danny first saw the officers, they quickly hid behind a tree. But it didn't help, as they had already been spotted.

"Now you two better come out", the tall man addressed them in a tone that demanded obedience. Katie and Danny slowly stepped forward.
"Why are you arresting us?" Katie wanted to know. "We haven't done anything wrong!"
"You think so?" the police officer put in.

"I don't just think so, I know it", Katie replied confidently.

"So you think there's nothing wrong with running away from school?" the man asked incredulously.

"We didn't run away", Katie explained. "We just walked out of the gate. And anyway, the teacher told me to leave."

"Of course, it's the teacher's fault!" the policeman laughed. "It's always the teachers' fault, never the children's!"

"Do you think so?" Katie looked up to him briefly.

The officer's face darkened. "Now don't start being cheeky!" he warned Katie. "You're dealing with the law."

Danny's hands began to flap and his nose started twitching, as it often did when he was under stress. "So you are arresting us?" he wanted to know.

"If you refuse to follow me, I can put you in hand cuffs." The policeman rattled the cuffs on his belt and stretched his other hand out towards Danny. That was enough to make him panic. Without thinking, Danny turned and sped away as fast as his legs would take him. The police officer didn't hesitate. He sprinted after him and with his long legs caught up with Danny in no time.

"Don't! Don't touch me!" Danny screamed, when the hand clamped down on his shoulder. Meanwhile, the other officer, a woman, had stepped forward.
"Please, make him let go", Katie begged her. "Danny can't stand being touched. It hurts him!"
The woman rushed to her colleague and said firmly: "Remember, they are autistic. Just let go of him. I've phoned the head

teacher and she will be here as soon as she can."

The man reluctantly let go of Danny and straightened up, mumbling: "Autistic or not, they have to learn their lesson."

It didn't take long for Mrs Macintyre to arrive with Miss Cotswold in tow.

"I'm so glad you're safe!" was the first she said and her whole being glowed with relief. "Come along, Katie and Danny! My car is in front of the Community Centre. I'll take you back to school."

The children followed her silently, while the police officers updated the station on their radios.

It was only as they came to the school gates that Katie suddenly stopped.

"What's wrong?" Miss Cotswold wanted to know. Katie hesitated. Then she asked in a trembling voice: "Are you sure I'm allowed back?"

Miss Cotswold looked confused. "Of course you are! You should never have left the school in the first place!"

"But the teacher told me to leave!" Katie reminded her. "She told me to seek my education elsewhere!"

Miss Cotswold sighed. "Don't be ridiculous! You're clever enough to know what she meant."

So this had been another of the teacher's riddles. If only people were saying what they meant, it would be so much easier to get on with each other, Katie thought.

5) Last Chance

Danny was surprised to find his dad waiting for him in the head teacher's office. He didn't look happy.

"Honestly, Danny, what were you thinking, running off like that!" his loud fireman's voice thundered through the room. "Anything could have happened to you out there!"

Danny put his hands in his pockets to stop them from flapping. His twitching nose, however, he couldn't control, so he faced the floor.

"It was a dangerous thing to do and I hope you will never repeat it", Mrs Macintyre added in a calmer voice. When Danny didn't answer, she asked: "Do you understand me?" Danny nodded, but that was obviously not good enough.

"Look at me!" Mrs Macintyre demanded. Danny lifted his head, but he couldn't meet her eyes. He found it impossible to look at people's eyes. It felt so intrusive and made it hard for him to take in what was being said.

"For goodness sake, Danny!" his dad broke the uncomfortable silence. "You could at least say that you are sorry! And stop that stupid twitching! It makes you look like a demented rabbit!"

"He can't help it", the head teacher came to his defence, "but your dad is right, you could at least apologise and promise to keep to the school rules."

Danny would have said so, only the words wouldn't form in his mouth. He was swaying from side to side, with his hands tearing at his trouser pockets and the twitching nose starting to hurt his face.

His dad sighed. "Fine then, no pocket money this week and no computer time either. If that's how you want it!"
Danny didn't care. In fact, he didn't really hear what his dad was saying. He heard his voice, but it sounded like a barking dog or a pounding hammer. He knew that he couldn't hold himself together much longer and would have agreed with anything to be allowed to leave.

"Come on then, get your school bag and we'll sort it out at home." His dad pushed him to the door. Outside the office Danny almost collided with Katie who had been waiting there with Miss Cotswold.

"Is it my turn?" she asked excitedly.

"I'd feel a bit more weary if I was you", Danny's dad told her. Miss Cotswold nodded in agreement. Then she beckoned Katie to follow her.

"What do you have to say for yourself?" Mrs Macintyre asked her when Katie was seated.

"What do you mean with *say for yourself?*" Katie tried to remember this figurative speech, but she couldn't find the right compartment in her brain.

"Listen, Katie, I'm giving you the chance to explain what happened from your point of view", Mrs Macintyre said impatiently.

"Alright, I get it", Katie replied. "The teacher told me to leave and to seek my education elsewhere, so I left."

"First of all, your teacher has a name", Mrs Macintyre interrupted. Katie began to fiddle with a button on her cardigan. "Yes, but I can never remember it", she admitted.

"It's Mrs Comiston-Straighter", the head teacher told her, "and it is high time you learned it, since most of the school year has already passed."

"Okay, but she told me to leave…"

"You'd better start from the beginning," Miss Cotswold interrupted her. "Tell Mrs Macintyre why Mrs Comiston-Straighter was angry with you. Go on!"

Katie didn't think this was relevant. The extracting of information had obviously been one of many misunderstandings she experienced every day. But being told to leave could surely only have one meaning.

"Perhaps Mrs Comiston-Straighter wanted you out of the classroom, but she would never have given you permission to leave the school", Mrs Macintyre insisted. "You are old enough to know that you are under no circumstances to get off the premises during the school day. It is one of our school rules."

"Well, we do go out sometimes", Katie kept her right. "We went to the church last Christmas and we went to sing in the Old Folks Home and when there's a fire drill we sometimes have to walk across to the Community Centre..."

The head teacher suddenly stood up, knocking some papers off her desk. "Stop being ridiculous, Katie! Do you always have to have the last word?" She sighed. "Here you are, a highly intelligent child and yet you don't seem to be able to follow the simplest of instructions!" She shook her head in frustration. "No matter what those professionals say about Autism, I think you're just having us on." She took a step forward. "And talking about school outings: If you want to go on the trip to the castle next week, your behaviour has to improve markedly. This is your last chance."

6) True Friends

As soon as Danny got home, he took off his school uniform. He hated the stiff shirt, the tight belt and the shoes encasing his feet. In fact, he hated all clothes apart from his flannel pyjamas into which he changed despite the fact that it was only early afternoon. His dad went back to bed, as he had to work another night shift at the fire station. Danny's brothers were still at school, but his dog, Rosie, was overjoyed to have company. She was full off energy, so Danny took her out in order to leave his dad in peace.

For the next half hour he threw sticks and balls for her in the garden and they wrestled with her rope toy. When they were out of breath, they crawled into the den Danny had built in the hedge at the bottom of the garden. It provided just enough space for the two of them cuddled up together. Rosie licked his hands, while Danny tickled her behind her ears. Rosie was the best friend he had ever had.

Looking back at the day, Danny began to wonder what it would be like to live with Rosie in the woods. Well, it would have to be a large forest with lots of interesting features. He imagined a steep cliff with a gushing waterfall that turned into a river, hurtling over rocks and boulders and teaming with fish. He dreamed of catching salmon and cooking them over an open fire. Rosie would hunt for rabbits and they would gather berries and mushrooms and maybe shoot a deer now and again.

"What do you think?" he asked Rosie. "Would you be happy living out there in the wild with me?"

Rosie was wagging her tail. Thinking of fishing and hunting gave Danny an idea. His dad had once made him a bow and arrows, but after a while he had lost them all and the bow got broken. However, Danny remembered how his dad had made it and he decided to build himself a new one.

For the next half hour he was absorbed in looking for the right wood and a piece of fishing line. Birch was best for the bow, because it was bendable. Danny managed to attach the piece of fishing line to it and to pull it tight. With a pair of garden scissors he cut half a dozen straight twigs and sharpened one end to turn them into arrows.

"Come on, Rosie! Let's go hunting!" Together they stalked through the garden like a Red Indian and his faithful hound. The trouble at school seemed a million miles away.

Katie had to wait until her mother picked her up from After School Club at half past four. Mrs Macintyre asked her into her office to discuss what had happened.

Katie's mum couldn't help laughing when she heard about the ripped out pages and Katie leaving the school at lunchtime. "It's just like her", she said. "She always takes you at your word."

Mrs Macintyre didn't find this in the least amusing. "She could have been attacked in the woods, a pretty girl like her", she put in. "And anyway, having to call a police search does not bode well for the reputation of the school."

Katie's mum looked up at her quizzically. "Are you afraid people will question the school's ability to cater for its autistic pupils?" she asked.

Mrs Macintyre shifted uncomfortably in her seat. "You know how hard we work to accommodate your daughter and other children like her", she said in defence. "You have to admit that it isn't easy to put up with her quirks, like ripping up library books to extract information."

"Of course, it's not easy for you", Katie's mum agreed, "but neither is it easy for Katie to understand what people mean. I thought that by now her teacher would have sussed out how her brain works."

Mrs Macintyre didn't like the way their conversation was heading, so she decided to bring it to a quick end. "I told Katie that she had one more chance to show responsibility for her actions or else I can't see how we can accommodate her on our class trip."

"Alright, I'll talk to her", Katie's mum promised. "And thank you for making sure she was found and returned safely." She stood up and shook hands, before leaving to collect her daughter.

Katie was skipping happily beside her mum. They had always got on well, because they were in many ways similar. Like Katie, her mother had suffered from misunderstandings throughout her life and had learned the hard way to find her place. She was now a lecturer in psychology and child development at the nearby university, but it had taken her many detours before reaching her goal.

At home Katie went straight to the piano. She let her fingers decide on the tunes they wanted to play and let herself be swept along by the music. Sometimes her mother joined in and they made up harmonies together without the use of words or books. In those moments Katie felt as if they became one person. Their fingers knew intuitively what was required of them to create a perfect expression of their feelings. It was like returning to the womb, where nothing had separated them. After all those misunderstandings in the big wide world, it was bliss to feel so connected.

"Soup's ready!" her mother called after a while. Katie finished the piece she was playing and went into the kitchen, where she was greeted by the familiar smell of freshly cooked vegetables.

7) Unsought Enemies

During the following days Danny and Katie tried very hard not to get into trouble at school. If only others hadn't tried so hard to get them into trouble!

"Look at those ancient bloomers!" Samantha shouted when the girls were changing for PE. "Handed down from your great-grandmother, are they?"

Katie looked at her underpants and then at Samantha's. Sure, hers were a lot bigger and covered quite a bit more of her body, but they were nice and comfortable. "My mum bought them for me", she said calmly. "I like them." The other girls were sniggering and Samantha made it clear that she wouldn't want to be seen dead in pants like that.

"Do you think you're going to die soon?" Katie asked somewhat concerned.

"You wish!" Samantha hissed at her. Then she put on her gym shoes and left for the hall.

After warm-up they were divided into teams for basketball. Katie liked to be physically active. She was a fast runner and quite good at gymnastics, but when it came to ball games she didn't exactly shine. The thing was, she didn't really care about winning and losing and the many different rules confused her. But she would try her best.

First her teammates ignored her and never let her have the ball. Katie soon felt bored and frustrated, when suddenly she saw her chance. She intercepted the ball, which was thrown to someone else, and dribbled it towards the basket.

"Here! Give it to me!" Samantha called, throwing her arms in the air. Katie would have liked to have a try at the basket, but too many children were standing in her way. So she passed the ball to Samantha, who immediately scored a goal.

"Yea!" all the players with a yellow bib cheered.

"You moron!"   "How can she be so daft!" "I knew she was bad luck", and other nasty expressions came from the players wearing red bibs. It was only then that Katie looked at the colour of her bib. She was in the red team. And she had just helped the yellow team to score a goal.

Samantha grinned triumphantly. Later in the changing room she couldn't stop bragging about her clever deceit. Katie knew she had been wronged and now she was being made fun of. It hurt her feelings. She didn't like to be called a moron. So she asked Samantha to stop.

"Why should I?" Samantha replied.

"Because I don't like it and it isn't fair", Katie answered truthfully.

"If you don't like it, then don't behave like an idiot!" Samantha told her.

"I'm not an idiot!" Katie shouted. "I'm much better at maths and spelling than you are and I'm the fastest girl in the class!"
Katie didn't understand why everybody started laughing at this. It was true. She was way ahead of the others in maths and spelling and could outrun every single one of them. Why were they laughing at her? Why did they always have to be so nasty? She grabbed her gym kit and fled.

Danny couldn't cope with the gym hall. The noise was too overwhelming and so he was allowed to run laps in the playground instead. On sunny days he usually enjoyed this, but when it was raining or gale force winds decided to attack him, he would rather have stayed indoors. Today it was calm and dry. A pale winter sun filtered through the branches of the trees and a flock of birds circled overhead. Danny spread out his arms, pretending to fly with them. So far the day had gone well and this afternoon a couple of science students were coming to explain more about their solar system. Danny had been looking forward to it all day.

When the teacher had taken the afternoon register, she said: "By the way, our expected visitors couldn't make it today. I'm trying to find another date for them."

Danny couldn't take it in. The teacher's words didn't make sense. Why were the visitors not able to come? It said on their timetable that they would be here by now, two students from university to share their findings about the solar system. Where were they?
The next announcement left him even more confused.

"Since I haven't prepared a science lesson, we'll do French instead", the teacher said.

"French?" Danny asked, as if the word described a disease and not a language. "But...but..."

"No buts! Lauren and Markus, give out the folders", the teacher interrupted him.

"I'm not doing French!" Danny shouted. "It says Science on the timetable, not French!"

The teacher sighed. "I've just explained that I'm not prepared for a science lesson. We have to accept that things can suddenly change and make the best of it."

"Well, I'm not prepared for a French lesson, so I'm not doing it!" Danny insisted. When Markus handed him the folder, Danny threw it on the floor.

"Danny!" the teacher warned him. "Pick that up at once or you can forget about the school trip next week!"

Reluctantly, Danny picked up his folder, but he was adamant not to engage with the lesson. It was wrong. The timetable said Science. They shouldn't be doing French.

Apart from little hick-ups like this and the incident in the changing room, Danny and Katie survived the rest of the week unscathed.

8) The Weekend

"Have you finished your homework?" Danny's mum asked him on Sunday night.

Danny didn't look up from the jigsaw puzzle he was working on. It was really tricky, 500 pieces and a lot of them making up the sky.

"Danny! I've asked you a question", his mum's voice got finally through to him.

"What?" he asked, still scanning the half finished picture in front of him to find the gap for the tiny blue piece in his hand.

"Have you finished your homework?" his mum called to him again. Danny mumbled something about not knowing what to do. He was so absorbed in the jigsaw puzzle that he couldn't remember what he had been given for homework.

"Go and get your school bag", his mum told him, but Danny wasn't listening. Whilst scanning the pieces in front of him, he had noticed two that definitely went together. He joined them up and put them to the side.

"Danny!" his mum shouted. "I said, go and get your school bag!" She grabbed him by the shoulder and pulled him to his feet.
"How many times do I have to say something before you can be bothered to do it?"

Danny shook her hand off. "I just need to finish the jigsaw puzzle", he told her, turning back to what he had been engrossed in, but his mum wouldn't leave him in peace.

"Listen, Danny, it's almost your bed time and I've told you again and again to get that homework done. This jigsaw can wait until tomorrow, but your homework can't", she said firmly. Danny, however, hadn't been listening. "Wow!" he exclaimed suddenly. "I've found it! Now I only need the bit with the eye..."

"For goodness sake, Danny, stop ignoring me!" His mum burst out next to him. "You get up right now and bring your school bag or else I'll put this jigsaw in the bin! Do you hear me?"

How could he not hear her, since she was screaming straight into his ear, but somehow her words didn't penetrate the bubble he was in. All that mattered at that moment was the emerging picture in front of him. He was completely focussed on putting the pieces together, each in their rightful place, and he couldn't stop until the task was completed. Had his two brothers not come in and asked for a drink, his mum might have lost her patience and carried out her threat.

"Can we have some hot chocolate?" Sean asked.
"We've tidied our bedroom and we've put our dirty clothes in the laundry basket", Callum added.

Their mum sighed. "Well done", she praised them and went to the kitchen to put the kettle on. "I wish Danny would follow your example."

But Danny wasn't listening. He hadn't even noticed his brothers entering the room. Only when Callum's hand reached for one of the jigsaw pieces, did he look up. "Hey, what are you doing?" he asked angrily.

"I'm trying to help you", Callum explained.

"Put it back! I don't need your help", Danny growled at him. Callum put the piece back, shrugged his shoulders and moved away.

It took Danny another twenty minutes to finish the jigsaw puzzle. He looked at the picture of the dog in the meadow, exhausted but pleased with himself. By then it was definitely time for bed, homework or no homework. Danny went to the bathroom, then stepped carefully over the toys littering his bedroom floor to reach the corner where he slept. His mum said good night to him from the door and switched the light off. Despite being so tired, it would take Danny about an hour to fall asleep.

Meanwhile, Katie had had a splendid weekend. On Saturday her mum had taken her to the beach, where the wind was whipping up the sea and sending waves crashing ashore. Despite the cold, they took their shoes and socks off and ran into the surf, shrieking with excitement.

On Sunday they went to church, singing and praying and listening to the minister talking about Jesus. Katie loved the atmosphere in the old church. The stained glass windows coming alive in the candle light gave her a sense of being in a different world, a world that revolved around God and where people became one with each other.
Later, they baked biscuits together and took them to an elderly neighbour, who was always overjoyed to see them.

Katie had done her homework as soon as it was given to her. Most of it she found easy, anyway. In her bedroom everything had its exact place. She would notice immediately if someone had moved an ornament in her shelf or one of the soft toys on her bed. Her books were all sorted in alphabetical order and her clothes lay neatly folded in her wardrobe. That's how Katie liked it: everything clear and ordered.

Once her cousin had stayed overnight in Katie's bedroom, while Katie had to share with her mum. Next morning, when Katie slipped in to get some clothes, she had been aghast finding that things were not in their rightful place. Although her cousin was still half asleep, Katie couldn't stop herself tidying up immediately.

"What's wrong?" her cousin wanted to know, rubbing her eyes and yawning.

"Everything's wrong!" Katie replied, hastily re-organising the stationary on her desk. Her cousin shook her head. "What does it matter if the rubber is next to the sharpener and not to the pencil?" she wanted to know.

"Because it's not the right place", Katie insisted. To her, there was a logical order, which mustn't be disturbed. Disorder was like misunderstandings; it was confusing and upsetting.

However, this weekend had been perfect and Katie was looking forward to the school trip on Wednesday.

9) Off to the Castle

The day arrived, when a big yellow bus drew up in front of the school gates and Mrs Comiston-Straighter was marching her class towards it. They all carried a packed lunch, as they wouldn't be back before the end of the school day.

Danny was one of the first children on the bus and slipped into the front seat, where he had the best view. He didn't mind that nobody wanted to sit beside him. At least he could travel in peace.
In the end he had to share with Katie, since she came last and all the other seats were taken either by children or their rucksacks.

Katie was very excited. She owed her inclusion in the trip to Mr Stuart, the

Depute Head, who had insisted that every child had the right to take part in educational excursions. Mrs Comiston-Straighter wasn't too happy with that, but she had to give in.

Being excited made Katie's body rock to and fro and she began to hum a soothing tune. Danny tried to block her out. He was watching the traffic flowing past, recognising the supermarket and the police station and finally the Animal Rescue Centre, where the countryside began. Fields with sheep and cattle gave way to long stretches of forest. They drove through a village, where someone was fixing a tractor, and saw a group on horseback, silhouetted against the shimmering sea. The pale winter sun was doing its best to break through the clouds, but mostly the sky looked grey.

Danny was trying to remember what was so special about Castle Lovat. After all, their current topic was *The Solar System*. Did the castle reach all the way into outer space? Danny chuckled at the thought of climbing thousands of steps and ending up in outer space.

Mrs Comiston-Straighter was glad that everyone was settled in their seats. She wouldn't have minded to spend the rest of the day on the bus with the countryside rolling past. In fact, the closer they came to their destination, the more she dreaded the visit to the castle.

"Who knows what that girl will be up to this time!" she voiced her concerns to Miss Cotswold. "She's made it her mission to show me up in front of the class. I dare not think about what havoc she'll wreak in those old ruins."

Miss Cotswold nodded. "You never know where you are at with Katie", she agreed. "You have to be so careful what you are saying, just like with Danny. You can never tell when and why the boy is flying off the handle."

Some of the children were also talking about Katie and Danny. Kyle was annoyed, because he felt Danny always got off lightly. "If I was throwing stuff around the room and telling Miss Cotswold to shut up, I'd be expelled", he complained.

Hassid agreed. "Sometimes he is like a ticking time bomb. Everybody's tiptoeing around him, afraid to set him off."

"And the cheek you get from Katie!" Vicky put in.

"Are you going to die soon?" Samantha mimicked what Katie had said to her in the changing room the other day. "Honestly, I don't know why she's allowed to come on the trip!"

However, the bus finally turned off into a single-track road and shortly after it passed under an enormous stone arch, leading into the castle grounds. The noise increased as they wound their way up a bumpy track framed by huge trees. Then came the shouts: "Look!"   "Wow!" "Awesome!" as the outline of the castle emerged in front of them. They had arrived.

"Remember what I said!" the teacher's voice boomed through the bus, when they had stopped. "You stay with your group at all times and listen carefully to the guide **and** do what he or she tells you. Is that clear?"

The children answered with a half-hearted "Yes, Mrs" and grabbed their bags, ready to get off.

Danny was in Miss Cotswold's group. They were assigned a young guide who introduced himself as Fraser and explained that he worked in the castle grounds. "I usually cut the grass, trim the hedges, fill the potholes in the track and do whatever needs doing to keep the place from turning back into a wilderness. But I also lead guided tours through the castle, which is what we're doing today."

The children followed him to the drawbridge, leading across an overgrown moat. "Once this was full of water", Fraser explained, "and I'll show you the place where Amelia Lovat fell in and drowned."

Mrs Comiston-Straighter's group was lead by an elderly lady, who was apparently a great-niece of the late Lord Lovat and lived in one of the old cottages in the castle grounds. She warned the children to be careful and not go off exploring, as the walls of the castle were crumbling and there were many dangerous pitfalls if they strayed off the beaten track.

"Who has beaten the track?" Katie wanted to know. Hassid and Vicky rolled their eyes and sighed.

"Shush, Katie!" the teacher hissed, but the great-niece of Lord Lovat didn't mind the question.

"The track was beaten by the feet of many a great man and woman", she said proudly. "After all, this castle is unique in the whole of Scotland, if not in the whole world." She led her group along the beaten track, veering to the opposite side of Fraser's group, once they had crossed the bridge and passed through the heavy wooden door.

10) Heroes of old

Danny was fascinated by the thick walls, the high ceilings and the small openings, which used to serve as windows or as positions for the archers. Like his classmates, he was impressed by the grand scale of the structure. But what he liked best where the many small hideouts and little turrets at the side of the building. He could imagine using one of them as a den for whenever he needed time by himself. The thick walls dampened the noise from the main halls, while the semi-darkness created a soothing atmosphere.

They stopped in front of a portrait gallery and Fraser began to talk about the various generations of Lovats who had lived in the castle.

"This here is Duncan Lovat who extended the castle in 1686", he told them, pointing to a grim looking man in a tartan outfit. "He later lost a leg in a horse riding accident, but it didn't hinder him carrying on leading his army into battle. He is said to have tied the stump of his missing leg to his saddle and off he rode in front of his men."

As if this wasn't impressive enough, Fraser stopped in front of another portrait, that of a young woman.
"This is Amelia Lovat in 1738, shortly before she drowned in the moat," he began. "She was a remarkable girl, highly gifted in music and poetry. In fact, some of her compositions have survived and are still being performed today."

Finally he led them to the portrait of a dishevelled looking man with huge eyes that were focussed somewhere in the distance.

"He looks crazy", Thomas whispered. "Like a psychopath or something."

Fraser must have heard him, because he explained that this man, Farquhar Lovat, had been a misfit and an embarrassment to his family from the day he was born. "He had no manners, but always blurted out what was on his mind. Even as a young boy he was known to interrupt adult conversation with his unusual questions, and instead of developing an interest in hunting or fighting or clan politics, he shut himself away at the top of the castle to gaze into space."

Now Danny remembered why they had chosen to visit this castle. It had played a crucial part in the modern understanding of the universe.

"Farquhar Lovat was a genius," Fraser went on to explain. "But like every genius, he would not fit in with the people around him. He was highly sensitive to sound, light and touch, but he didn't show any sensitivity when it came to telling people what he thought. The truth was more important to him than social niceties." He cleared his throat, before adding rather thoughtfully: "I think nowadays he would have said to be autistic."

Danny's heart skipped a beat when he heard this. He stared at his feet, as he felt many pairs of eyes turning in his direction. Perhaps one day he would become famous like Farquhar Lovat. Perhaps being autistic wasn't all bad.

Meanwhile Katie's group was standing at the bottom of a spiral staircase, leading up to the highest point of the castle.

"In a moment you will come to the most notable part of this castle", their guide explained. "It was only added in the 1820s by the youngest son of James Lovat, whose portrait you saw earlier in the gallery."

"The crazy guy?" Kyle asked, ignoring the disapproving look of his teacher.

"Some people sought him to be crazy, but what he found out has changed the whole understanding of astrology", Lovat's great-niece answered. "Now follow me, but be careful, the steps are very steep."

They wound their way up the narrow spiral staircase until they arrived in a round room covered by a dome of dirty glass. A broad window ledge ran across the perimeter of the room, leaving little space for the children to stand.

"Welcome to Farquhar Lovat's study", the guide announced, "where he shut himself away from the world for almost thirty years."

"Thirty years?" someone piped up.

"Yes", the guide nodded. "The servants would come up every day to bring him food and empty his toilet bucket. They also brought him water to wash and fresh clothes, but he didn't care much about his body. All that mattered to him was to unravel the mysteries of the stars and the planets. And he made some amazing discoveries." She opened a folder and showed them carefully laminated pages of handwritten sketches and complicated mathematical equations.

Katie stepped forward and stared at the figures and numbers.

"By carefully observing the constellations of the night sky, measuring distance and noting angles, he was able to predict the exact time and place of a meteor shower or the sighting of a comet. He could tell when a new star was born and when to expect a lunar eclipse." She was so enthralled by her ancestor and his discoveries, that she hardly noticed the shuffling and yawning of her audience. Only Katie showed enthusiasm, as she was able to detect patterns in the mathematical scribbles.

"I get it!" she suddenly burst out, making the guide stop in mid-sentence. "The longer the distance between two stars, the narrower the angle in relation to our planet!" Katie beamed with joy and pride at this discovery. "Can I see the next page, please?"

The other children began to sigh and roll their eyes. The shuffling of their feet became louder and their whispers and murmurs grew into noisy complaints. In the end, Mrs Comiston-Straighter clapped her hands and shouted: "Shush! Quiet now! Mind your manners, children!"

The guide suddenly realised that she had lost most of her audience and summed up her talk about Farquhar Lovat by praising him for being the for-runner of modern astrology and astro-physics. "He insisted that there must be a Higher Power behind this amazingly organised solar system, where every tiny detail has its exact place and meaning." She lifted her head and let her eyes wander across the faces in front of her.

"That, children, is pure genius. Only single-minded dedication can achieve such depth of understanding. So don't call Farquhar Lovat a crazy man. Outwardly he might have looked crazy, but his achievements showed that inside he was a highly gifted person. He was one of the heroes of this castle."

11) Going too far

Samantha, Kyle and Vicky were the first to descent the spiral staircase.

"Can't see what makes that crazy loon a hero", Kyle mumbled.

"Yea, what's so important about comets and meteors?" Vicky put in.

"Unless you're Katie", Samantha chuckled and mimicked Katie's voice: "The longer the distance of the stars, the brighter they shine in the sky, ha ha ha!"

"She's just as crazy as that Farquhar Lovat", Kyle put in.

"Which means she's a genius", Vicky figured.

"And a hero, of course!" Samantha added.

They carried on making fun of Katie, when Kyle suddenly noticed a niche at the side of the main walkway. He climbed over a rope, which cordoned it off, and leaned out through a hole in the thick wall.

"There's a ledge out there, a kind of balcony", he reported to the other two. "Hey, you can stand out there and enjoy the grand view!"

"We're not supposed to go in here", Vicky said wearily. "This place is roped off."

"Who cares! Let me see, Kyle!" Samantha pushed past her and Kyle drew back from the window to make room for her.

"Wow! Not bad!" she commented. "A pedestal for a hero!" That suddenly gave her an idea. "We should get Katie to stand there. That would be really heroic, not like stupid maths stuff."

Just then they heard the other children come along, led by the teacher with Katie and the guide bringing up the rear. Kyle quickly ducked into a corner and Samantha grabbed Vicky to hide with her. The procession went past without a glimpse in their direction. They could have stayed in their hiding place and followed the group at some distance, but when Samantha saw Katie with a big smile on her face, she felt unable to resist. Knowing that Katie often heard sounds that for other people were inaudible, she whispered her name.

Katie stopped and looked around.

"Here! We're here!" Samantha guided her with her voice. Katie hesitated for a moment. The group disappeared round the corner and she knew that she ought to stay with the others. But why was Samantha calling her name? Did she need help? Or had she made an amazing discovery and needed Katie to figure out what it meant? After all, she had been the only one to understand Farquhar Lovat's mathematical equations. So she stepped over the rope and met with Samantha and her two friends.

"We've found the ideal place for you to stand," Samantha greeted her. "Come here!" She waved Katie over to the gap in the wall and told her to crawl in.

"See that balcony?" she asked when Katie was leaning out.

"Yes", Katie said, "but it hasn't got banisters and it's pretty high up."

"You can see the dome of the observatory from standing out there", Samantha told her.

"Really?" Katie asked.

"Yea, it's awesome", Samantha encouraged her. "Never mind that there isn't a banister. The ledge's wide enough to stand comfortably and you can hold on to the wall." She made it sound so easy, that Katie pushed away her fears and carefully crawled through the hole and out onto the balcony.

Vicky held her breath. Then she asked: "What if she falls down? She'd die!"

"And?" Samantha said gleefully. "What's one loony less!"

Kyle shuffled on the spot. He didn't like what was going on. Katie might be a bit weird, but that was no reason to send her to her death. He suddenly made up his mind. Pushing past Samantha, he followed Katie through the hole in the wall and called: "Come back! I'll give you a hand."

Katie was slowly getting to her feet. She held on to the wall and looked up. With the clouds sailing past, she suddenly felt dizzy. So she looked down instead, but that only made her feel worse. Then the stone under her left foot began to crumble. Katie let out a shriek of horror and shuffled further to the right. The stone she had been standing on crashed all the way to the ground.

"Oh no!" Kyle screamed.

"What's happened?" Samantha wanted to know.

"The balcony! It's breaking!" Kyle stretched out his arm, but Katie was beyond his reach. "Go and get help, quickly!" he shouted.

Vicky was already on her way. She ran after the group, screaming for help, while Samantha was following her, saying over and over again: "I didn't mean it! It was just a joke!"

Katie forced herself to breathe slowly in and out. She kept her eyes on the wall in front of her with her fingers clawing at the rough stone. She knew that to panic would lead to certain death, so she began to hum a song that she knew from Assembly.

"Jesus loves me, this I know,
For the Bible tells me so;
All our lives to God belong;
I am weak, but He is strong."

On and on she hummed the soothing tune to stay calm until help would arrive.

12) The Rescue

The guide and the teacher had difficulty understanding what the girls were trying to say. They had arrived at the entrance, where Fraser was already waiting with his group.

"Slow down, girls, and tell us one at a time what has happened", Mrs Comiston-Straighter demanded.

"You have to come quickly before she falls!" Vicky cried in response.

It was Fraser who acted first. "Show me where she is", he told the girls. Samantha and Vicky ran back up the stairs, followed by Fraser and pursued by a mop of children with the other adults in tow.

They were out of breath when they reached Kyle in the alcove.

"Here! She's out here!" Kyle pointed through the narrow opening. Fraser rushed forward and stuck his head through the gap. "Oh my word!" they heard him sigh. One look was enough to let him know how desperate the situation was.

"Call the fire brigade!" he shouted to the group behind him.

"They take at least twenty minutes to get here", the older guide replied. "Do we have enough time?"

"Part of the ledge has already broken off", Kyle shouted almost hysterical. "The rest can crumble any time!"

Fraser quickly assessed the situation. Kyle was right. There was no time to lose. He scanned the wall above the ledge and spotted a similar window about eight to ten metres higher. He quickly drew back into the alcove. "We need a rope", he said.

"There's that long cord at the back of the maintenance cupboard", the older guide replied. Fraser pushed past the children and rushed down the stairs to fetch it.

"Who's out there?" Danny wanted to know.

"I think it's Katie", Callum answered. "Don't ask me how she got there. Must be one of her crazy ideas."

"Katie's not crazy!" Danny defended his friend.

"Well, she acts crazy half of the time", Callum insisted. Danny wound his way to the front, trying his best to avoid brushing against the other children.

"Is Katie out there?" he asked when he reached his teacher. Kyle answered instead of her. "She's standing on a ledge and a bit has already broken off." He could no longer hold his tears back. How could they have lured her into this trap? He leaned his head against the wall and cried unashamedly.

Danny leaned out through the gap to see for himself where Katie was standing. He heard her humming softly and knew that for the moment she was all right, but it was clear that she couldn't get back where the ledge was broken. He looked up and saw the window above. Immediately he understood what Fraser had in mind. He drew back and stepped out onto the staircase, where the group had parted to let Fraser through with the coil of rope over his shoulder. Danny followed him, before the teacher turned the children back.

"You all go down to the driveway and wait for the bus!" she told them in her usual teacher's voice. "You'll only be in the way up here." She shooed them down like a flock of sheep, while the older guide hurried after Fraser and Danny.

Within seconds they reached the narrow window above the ledge where Katie was trapped. Fraser saw at once that the opening wasn't wide enough for a grown man like himself.

"I know how to abseil", Danny volunteered. "My dad has taught me. I know what to do."

Fraser looked at him, considering for a moment how to proceed. They didn't really have an option. Any minute the rest of the ledge could break off or Katie could simply lose her nerve and fall.

"Ok, lift up your arms", he instructed Danny. With nimble fingers he tied the rope round his waist. Danny crawled through the opening. For a moment he was suspended upside down above the huge drop. In the distance he could see the bus rumbling up the drive like a toy in a miniature world. His stomach lurched and his bladder wanted to open, but he didn't give in to those feelings of dread. Instead, he kicked off from the window and let the rope righten him again. Then he pressed his feet against the wall and called out to Fraser above: "Ready to lower!"

The rest of the class had gathered on the verge of the driveway. Every pair of eyes was focussed on the two children high up the castle wall, one standing on a tiny ledge, while the other was slowly proceeding towards her. Nobody spoke a word. It was as if they were all holding their breath, including the teacher who thought this might be the end of her career.

Meanwhile Danny was steadily 'walking down' the castle wall until he dangled beside Katie. The next bit was the hardest part of the rescue. They hadn't really discussed how to go about it, but seeing Katie and the state she was in, Danny knew what he had to do. He took her by the hand and said calmly: "I'll put you on the rope above me. When you're ready and on the way, I'll tie myself off and wait on the ledge, while Fraser is pulling you up."

Katie didn't respond. It was hard to tell whether she had understood him. Perhaps she had withdrawn into her inner world where she felt safe and calm. Danny placed his feet on either side of her and called to Fraser to give him some slack on the rope. He then made a loop around Katie's waist, fastening it with the knots his dad had shown him. Finally he loosened the knot around his own waist and called up: "Ready to pull!"

Their roles were reversed. Instead of Katie, it was now Danny's turn to stand on the crumbling ledge. He felt detached from his body, as if he was looking down on himself from a safe place. This feeling wasn't new to him. He had often experienced it before, when things had become too frightening or too painful. Perhaps it was one of the advantages his autism gave him. It certainly served him well, whilst waiting for Katie to be pulled to safety, before the rope was lowered again to help him back up.

Fraser's forehead was dripping with sweat, when he finally helped Danny back into the building. Katie was wrapped into the older guide's arms. She still appeared to be in shock, with her eyes staring into the faraway distance. Danny untied the knot and let the rope drop to his feet. He slowly walked over to Katie and said: "The bus has come. It's time to go home."

When the four of them stepped out onto the drawbridge, a huge round of applause went up from the crowd that had watched them. Even the bus driver joined in, shouting: "Hooray to the heroes!"

Danny automatically put his hands over his ears to dampen the painful noise. He turned to look for the fateful ledge, but he couldn't make it out. Perhaps it had collapsed completely.

Mrs Comiston-Straighter did her best to quieten the children on the bus, but in the end it was the driver's threat to make them walk home that reined in their excitement. As soon as they arrived at the school gates, the cacophony started up again, until every single pupil, teacher and picking-up parent knew what had happened at the castle. One of the parents was a journalist, hungry for a catching story. By the next morning it would be the talk of the town.

13) Aftermaths

Kyle couldn't sleep that night. Whenever he closed his eyes, he saw the piece of balcony breaking off and crashing down into the abyss. He heard Katie's scream and felt his heart stop. Something had changed in him at that moment. Until then it had just been a joke like the many other jokes they had played on Katie over the years. It had been funny to see her do exactly what they asked her to. She was so naïve, so gullible. Again and again she fell into the trap they set for her. Why didn't she grasp what was going on? How could she not get it? It didn't make sense for someone so bright when it came to maths or science. And they had all enjoyed making fun of her. They had all laughed at her expense and never stopped to think what it might feel like to her.

But at that moment, when the ancient stones of the castle had begun to shift, something had shifted in Kyle, too. He had suddenly realised where their cruel jokes were leading. Katie took people by their word. She believed what they were saying and in her innocence she didn't figure out when people were leading her astray. How many times had they got her into trouble or reduced her to tears, just for the fun of seeing her suffer! And this might be the last time, the culmination of all the years of cruelty. If Katie fell off that ledge, it would be like murder. So many times had they pushed her over the edge, but this would be the last time. There was no way back; it was final.

On the way back from the castle, Mrs Comiston-Straighter and Miss Cotswold had enough to do, trying to calm the children. Katie was in a kind of daze, so they left her to recover. When they had arrived at school, it was home time. Kyle had seen Vicky and Samantha sneak away, deep in whispered conversation like a couple of thieves hatching out their next robbery. It didn't take much imagination to guess what they were up to. Kyle knew that the incident wasn't just over and dealt with. Katie had nearly died out there and the teacher would want to know why she had been on that ledge in the first place. Everybody knew of her crazy impulses, but they also knew that she would never lie. That's why Vicky and Samantha were hatching out a plan to keep themselves out of trouble. But Kyle wasn't going along with that. He had gone along with the others for far too long. It was time to be brave and to stand up for the truth, whatever that would mean for him.

The next morning Kyle arrived early at school. He rang the bell at reception, fiddling nervously with the zip of his jacket. The secretary had not yet arrived. Instead, the head teacher opened the door for him and led him straight into her office.

"I'm glad you've come early", she said, offering him a seat. "Mrs Comiston-Straighter told me about the incident yesterday at the castle and she mentioned that you had been first at the scene and sent the two girls to ring the alarm."

Kyle swallowed and nodded. It would be easy to pretend that he had found Katie by accident and then take credit for his swift actions. But it wasn't the truth. It would leave Katie to explain why she had climbed out in the first place, and if Samantha and Vicky denied having lured her there, it would make Katie look even crazier. They might expel her from school. They might even put her in a psychiatric hospital to keep her safe. No, he had to tell the truth, whatever the consequences were for him and the two girls.

Once Kyle had started, he was not to be stopped. He told Mrs Macintyre everything that had led to Katie finding herself trapped on the crumbling ledge. He didn't deny his own involvement. He could have stopped Samantha. He could have held Katie back. But he didn't. He was as guilty as she and Vicky were and he felt thoroughly ashamed of himself. It didn't matter that the head teacher saw him sobbing his heart out. He no longer had anything to lose.

Mrs Macintyre got up to fetch a couple of tissues and handed them to Kyle. She was too shocked about what he had told her to offer her comments. Could children in her school really be so cruel to one of their peers? She took a deep breath. The worst was that she could well understand what made it so tempting to bully Katie in this way. What was it about the girl that she was able to grasp the most intricate mathematical problems but couldn't distinguish between hoax and reality? Perhaps they all had a lesson to learn from this shocking incident. They all needed a better understanding of what it means to be autistic.

Kyle was not being expelled for his part in luring Katie into danger; neither were Vicky or Samantha. But all three of them had to live with the shame and guilt for what they had done. It was worse than being expelled, for soon the whole school knew what had happened, and while Danny was celebrated for his heroic rescue, Kyle, Vicky and Samantha were treated like outcasts. The girls had at least each other, but for Kyle having no one to hang out with was a new experience. After moping around for a week or two, he could bear it no longer. At playtime he approached a group of boys from his class and said: "I know I messed up big time with Katie at the castle, but I'm truly sorry." He looked from one to the other before adding: "And I can still kick a ball around, you know?" With that he stepped forward and tackled the boy who had brought a football, getting the better of him and racing towards the goal. The spell was broken. The boys raced after him and Kyle was once more part of their game.

Danny couldn't decide whether he liked the new attention he got or not. After appearing on the front page of the local newspaper, suddenly everyone wanted to be his friend. First he sunned himself in the praise, but it didn't take long before it was all getting too much for him and he preferred to pace along the playground fence by himself and enjoy the freedom of letting his hands flap and his nose twitch without anyone commenting on it.

It took Katie almost an hour at the piano after returning home from the castle, before she was able to face the world again. She told her mum what had happened and they had a long conversation about keeping yourself safe.

"People can be cruel and deceiving", her mum warned her. "They sometimes lie to make you do dangerous things. You always have to think for yourself: Is this a good idea? If not, say no and walk away."

Katie nodded, but her mum knew that she still had a long way to go to figure out other people's intentions.

14) Happier Times

Mrs Macintyre had not forgotten about her intention to gain a better understanding of her autistic pupils. In the end it was Katie's mum who pointed her in the right direction. She knew of a group of autistic adults who led workshops for school staff and pupils, sharing their own experience and what worked for them. Their workshop was called "Insight into Autism" and it started off like this:

> "Imagine you were the only English-speaking student in a class of Polish kids and they don't know why you cannot understand them...

Imagine you were suffering from a dreadful toothache, yet the teacher expects you to get on with your work like everybody else...

Imagine there were three different television programmes on side-by-side and you have to listen to the one in the middle...

Imagine your mind was geared and ready for a maths lesson, but instead the teacher goes on and on about the Roman invasion...

Imagine you have just made a really exciting discovery, but when you try to share it, nobody shows any interest or understanding...

How would you feel?

Frustrated? Angry? Left out? Lonely? Confused? Overwhelmed? Scared?

Like an alien on the wrong planet?

For many autistic children the social use of language can feel like a foreign tongue, but unlike Polish or French other people don't usually offer to translate, explain or simplify what has been said.

A lot of autistic people suffer intolerable pain from sensory stimuli which other people might not even notice, like the buzzing of ceiling lights, the background noise of electronic equipment or even the ticking of a wall clock. We all know how difficult it is to function, never mind work, when we are in pain.

Autistic people often have very unique interests and pleasures and don't understand the purpose and rules of the games their peers are engrossed in.

Of course, we all have to bear with subjects and topic that don't interest us, but for autistic people things have to be relevant or else we can't make sense of them, and once we're geared for maths, we can't just shift over to history.

The biggest advantage of autism is single-mindedness. I know, to be engrossed in the Jacobite Risings or to identify every single dinosaur by its Latin name does not sound very useful. It's often seen as an obsession that gets on other people's nerves. But without that single-mindedness we wouldn't have had the sort of discoveries and inventions that have been made over the centuries."

The following weeks saw some major changes at school. Some of the wall displays in the classroom were removed and Danny got his own desk in a corner where he was less distracted. Mrs Comiston-Straighter slowly improved at explaining things to Katie, which left no room for misunderstandings. But the greatest change involved the attitude of the other children. They would never forget watching Danny and Katie high up on the castle wall. They would forever remember their bravery. Katie and Danny might be acting strangely at times, like that Farquhar Lovat with his observatory on top of the castle, but they deserved as much respect as anyone else.

The last day before the Easter holidays Callum came up to Danny and said: "I'm getting a puppy, an Irish Setter cum Labrador."

"They're lovely", Danny replied.

"Yes", Callum agreed, "but my parents said I have to train him. I thought, maybe you can help me, since you know about dogs."

Danny considered this for a minute. He had never met up with any of his classmates outside school. Would it feel too intrusive, having Callum and his puppy around? On the other hand he was curious about the dog. "I wonder what Rosie makes of him", he thought aloud.

"So I can come round some time?" Callum asked hopeful.

"Yes, I'll be around", Danny replied, still unsure about the new experience.

Katie would not be around in the holidays. For the first time, her mum had booked her on a Christian Youth Camp. Katie only agreed to go when she learned that there was a Steinberg piano and that she was expected to play it every day to accompany the singing. She packed her five favourite soft toys but forgot socks and underwear. Just as well her mum was checking her bag before she left.